my itty-bitty bio

Robert Fulton

Published in the United States of America by Cherry Lake Publishing
Ann Arbor, Michigan
www.cherrylakepublishing.com

Content Adviser: Jessica Criales, Doctoral Candidate, History Department, Rutgers University
Reading Adviser: Marla Conn MS, Ed., Literacy specialist, Read-Ability, Inc.
Book Design: Jennifer Wahi
Illustrator: Jeff Bane

Photo Credits: ©Delmas Lehman/Shutterstock, 5; ©Nomad_Soul/Shutterstock, 7; ©tsuneomp/Shutterstock, 9, 22; ©Everett Historical/Shutterstock, 11; ©AVA Bitter/Shutterstock, 13; ©Kostyantyn Ivanyshen/Shutterstock, 15; ©Everett Historical/Shutterstock, 17, 23; ©Everett Historical/Shutterstock, 19; ©Everett Historical/Shutterstock, 21; Cover, 6, 8, 14, Jeff Bane; Various frames throughout, ©Shutterstock Images

Copyright ©2019 by Cherry Lake Publishing
All rights reserved. No part of this book may be reproduced or utilized in any form or by any means without written permission from the publisher.

Library of Congress Cataloging-in-Publication Data

Names: Marsico, Katie, 1980- author.
Title: Robert Fulton / by Katie Marsico.
Description: Ann Arbor, Michigan : Cherry Lake Publishing, [2018] | Series: My itty-bitty bio | Includes bibliographical references and index. | Audience: Grades K-3.
Identifiers: LCCN 2018003266| ISBN 9781534128903 (hardcover) | ISBN 9781534130609 (pdf) | ISBN 9781534132108 (pbk.) | ISBN 9781534133808 (hosted ebook)
Subjects: LCSH: Fulton, Robert, 1765-1815--Juvenile literature. | Marine engineers--United States--Biography--Juvenile literature. | Inventors--United States--Biography--Juvenile literature. | Steamboats--Juvenile literature.
Classification: LCC VM140.F9 M375 2018 | DDC 623.82/4092 [B] --dc23
LC record available at https://lccn.loc.gov/2018003266

Printed in the United States of America
Corporate Graphics

table of contents

My Story 4

Timeline 22

Glossary 24

Index 24

About the author: Katie Marsico is the author of more than 200 reference books for children and young adults. She lives with her husband and six children near Chicago, Illinois.

About the illustrator: Jeff Bane and his two business partners own a studio along the American River in Folsom, California, home of the 1849 Gold Rush. When Jeff's not sketching or illustrating for clients, he's either swimming or kayaking in the river to relax.

my story

I was born in Pennsylvania.
I dreamed of being an artist.

I wanted to paint **portraits**.

Later, I traveled to Europe.
My art didn't sell well.

But I had an idea.

Where would you like to travel?

I pictured a ship like no other. It moved under the water.

It sped toward the ocean floor. I planned the first working **submarine**!

I returned to the United States.

I began building a steamboat. This was a boat with a **steam engine**.

What would you like to build?

The steam engine was an important **invention**!

Someone else invented the steam engine. I used it to make ships better.

Before, wind moved ships.
So did the flow of water.

Travel was slower.

My steamboat used machine power. Travel time sped up.

It made travel easier.

My steamboat changed the world.

People moved goods more quickly. This was better for trade.

How will you change the world?

I died in 1815. I did important work.

I gave people a new way to travel on the water.

What would you like to ask me?

timeline

1804

1760

↑
Born
1765

1807

1860

Died
1815

glossary & index

glossary

engine (EN-juhn) a machine that uses power to make something move

invention (in-VEN-chuhn) some useful thing that is newly made

portraits (POR-trits) drawings of people, usually just their faces

steam (STEEM) the gas that water turns into when it boils

submarine (SUHB-muh-reen) a ship built to travel under the water

index

art, 4, 6

invention, 8, 10, 12

ship, 8, 12, 14
steam engine, 10, 12
steamboat, 10, 16, 18
submarine, 8

travel, 6, 14, 16, 18, 20